"HELLO READING books are a perfect introduction to reading. Brief sentences full of word repetition and full-color pictures stress visual clues to help a child take the first important steps toward reading. Mastering these storybooks will build children's reading confidence and give them the enthusiasm to stand on their own in the world of words."

—Bee Cullinan
Past President of the International Reading
Association, Professor in New York University's
Early Childhood and Elementary Education Program

"Readers aren't born, they're made. Desire is planted—planted by parents who work at it."

—Jim Trelease
author of *The Read-Aloud Handbook*

"When I was a classroom reading teacher, I recognized the importance of good stories in making children understand that reading is more than just recognizing words. I saw that children who have ready access to storybooks get excited about reading. They also make noticeably greater gains in reading comprehension. The development of the HELLO READING stories grows out of this experience."

—Harriet Ziefert
M.A.T., New York University School of Education
Author, Language Arts Module,
Scholastic Early Childhood Program

For Amy, Jon, and Sam

VIKING
Published by the Penguin Group
Penguin Books USA Inc.,
375 Hudson Street, New York, New York 10014, U.S.A.
Penguin Books Ltd, 27 Wrights Lane, London W8 5TZ, England
Penguin Books Australia Ltd, Ringwood, Victoria, Australia
Penguin Books Canada Ltd, 10 Alcorn Avenue, Toronto, Ontario, Canada M4V 3B2
Penguin Books (N.Z.) Ltd, 182-190 Wairau Road, Auckland 10, New Zealand

Penguin Books Ltd, Registered Offices: Harmondsworth, Middlesex, England

First published in 1992 by Viking Penguin, a division of Penguin Books USA Inc.

Published simultaneously in a Puffin Books edition.

1 3 5 7 9 10 8 6 4 2

Text copyright © Fred Ehrlich, 1992
Illustrations copyright © Martha Gradisher, 1992
All rights reserved
Library of Congress Catalog Card Number: 91-48451
ISBN: 0-670-84651-1

Printed in Singapore for Harriet Ziefert, Inc.

A CLASS PLAY WITH MS. VANILLA

Fred Ehrlich
Pictures by Martha Gradisher

VIKING

Ms. Vanilla's class is happy today.
We are about to do a play.

The whole school is sitting there.
"Open the curtain!"
says Mr. Blair.

"Our story begins in a house by the wood.

It's the tale of Little Red Riding Hood."

"Take this basket,
Little Red Riding Hood,
To Granny's house
Through the big, dark wood."

"I'll sing as I walk from tree to tree.
No wolf would dare take a bite of me."

"Did you know that trees can worry?

We wish Red Riding Hood would hurry."

"We are the hunters
Who sing a song,
And carry our guns
As we march along."

"I'm the wolf. I'm mean, they say.
I want to eat everyone in the play.
I tied Granny behind the bed.
Now I'm waiting for Little Red."

"What big eyes you have!"
says Red Riding Hood.
"Granny, you don't look so good."

"What big teeth you have!"
says Red Riding Hood.
"Granny, you don't look so good."

"It's not your Granny in the bed.
I'll eat you now!" the mean wolf sa

"Look out, you wolf,
You're not so smart.
We've been watching you
From the start."

"We'll grab your tail.
We'll pull your paws.
We'll save Granny
From your jaws."

"Now that Granny's free at last,

We'd like to show you our whole cast."

"And just to make
  Our play a thriller,
  The horrible wolf is…

" Ms. Vanilla! "

DATE DUE			

E
EHR

Ehrlich, Fred.

A class play with Ms. Vanilla.

**WILLOW GROVE SCHOOL
LEARNING CENTER**